STEP INTO READING® will help your child get there. The program offers five steps to reading success. Each step includes fun stories and colorful art or photographs. In addition to original fiction and books with favorite characters, there are Step into Reading Non-Fiction Readers, Phonics Readers and Boxed Sets, Sticker Readers, and Comic Readers—a complete literacy program with something to interest every child.

Learning to Read, Step by Step!

Ready to Read   Preschool–Kindergarten
• big type and easy words • rhyme and rhythm • picture clues
For children who know the alphabet and are eager to begin reading.

Reading with Help   Preschool–Grade 1
• basic vocabulary • short sentences • simple stories
For children who recognize familiar words and sound out new words with help.

Reading on Your Own   Grades 1–3
• engaging characters • easy-to-follow plots • popular topics
For children who are ready to read on their own.

Reading Paragraphs   Grades 2–3
• challenging vocabulary • short paragraphs • exciting stories
For newly independent readers who read simple sentences with confidence.

Ready for Chapters   Grades 2–4
• chapters • longer paragraphs • full-color art
For children who want to take the plunge into chapter books but still like colorful pictures.

STEP INTO READING® is designed to give every child a successful reading experience. The grade levels are only guides; children will progress through the steps at their own speed, developing confidence in their reading.

Remember, a lifetime love of reading starts with a single step!

Visit us on the Web!
Seussville.com
StepIntoReading.com
rhcbooks.com

Educators and librarians, for a variety of teaching tools, visit us at RHTeachersLibrarians.com

Library of Congress Cataloging-in-Publication Data is available upon request.
ISBN 978-0-593-56914-6 (trade) — ISBN 978-0-593-56915-3 (lib. bdg.)

Printed in the United States of America
10 9 8 7 6 5 4 3 2 1

COOKING
with the
BIRTHDAY
BIRD

by Glenda Armand
illustrated by Jan Gerardi

Random House ⌂ New York

The Birthday Bird flew
from Katroo.

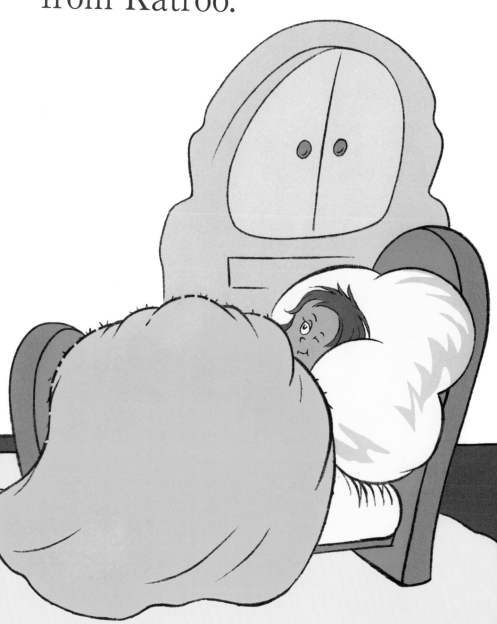

He will bake

a cake for you!

Just for you!

This is your day!

He will bake
the Katroo way.

He has a book.

Take a look!

Grab a hat!

Help him cook.

Sugar, flour.

Add milk, too.

Now crack some eggs.
Just two will do.

15

Now you mix it.
Spin! Spin! Spin!

Look!

You have some
on your chin!

Let it bake . . .

and then cool down.

Squeeze on pink

and blue and brown.

Now he will sing
the birthday song.

This is your day
so sing along!

You eat your cake.

You dance and play.

Now the Birthday Bird
must fly away . . .

. . . until next year
on your Big Day!